Windmill

Granny
Rabbit's cottage

The Squirrels
lived in these woods

This is the hill
they whizzed
down

They gathered
flowers here

Frankie
Frog's house

Mr Mole's
house

Freda
Fieldmouse's
cottage

Hedgehog's
house

Tasseltip has a lucky day

Story by Sarah Cotton
Illustrations by
Ernest A. Aris and Roy Smith

*Based on the original characters
created by Dorothy Richards*

Ladybird Books Loughborough

TASSELTIP'S LUCKY DAY

At the beginning of the week Mr Hare had stuck a large poster in the window of the shop at Hedgerow Corner to say that the annual Flower Show was to be held on Saturday in Deep Wood.

Amongst other things there was to be a Wild Flower Competition, and Tasseltip and many of his friends decided to enter. Early in the morning on the day of the show they were all busy in the fields picking as many flowers as they could find.

"Look at my bunch, Frankie," said Tasseltip proudly, holding them up for his friend to see.

"It's huge," replied Frankie, impressed.

"Oh! look what else I've found!" said Tasseltip. He ran to where a wild rose bush was growing. It was simply covered in bright red, fairy pin cushions. As he began to pick some, Susie Squirrel saw him.

"They are lovely," she said happily. "Save some for me," and she pushed her way nearer.

"Be careful," cried Tasseltip, but it was too late. He lost his balance and toppled backwards into the bush, and his huge bunch of flowers fell out of his paw!

Tasseltip struggled and struggled to free himself until Robert Rat came to his rescue. Laughing at his friend's plight he said, "What an uncomfortable place to choose to sit in. Mind those thorns or they will scratch you," and he stretched out his paw to pull Tasseltip up. "Are you all right?"

"I think so," replied Tasseltip, brushing himself down. "Oh no! My flowers! They are everywhere."

When Tasseltip had fallen into the rose bush he had dropped his flowers and now the wind had scattered them in every direction.

"Tasseltip, I am most dreadfully sorry," said Susie miserably. "You must take these," and she thrust her own bunch of flowers into Tasseltip's paws.

"Susie, that is very, very kind of you," said Tasseltip giving them back to her. "But I can't accept. You keep your flowers and I will pick some more."

The two friends smiled at each other and Tasseltip went off to pick a new bunch of flowers. This time, he kept his eyes wide open all the time so as not to bump into anyone else.

 It wasn't long before he had collected a new bunch of flowers and he decided to go home and show them to his mother.

She was amazed at the amount he had picked. "They are really lovely," said Mrs Rabbit. "I'll get you a vase when I have finished the ironing," she went on. "I won't be very long. Leave them on the table, and I will see to them."

But Tasseltip was far too impatient to wait. He noticed that there was a rather pretty vase on the mantelpiece, but he was too small to reach it, even when standing on tip-toe. He took a chair from the table and placed it under the shelf, then climbed on to it. He still couldn't reach the vase. He looked around and saw his stool in the corner. He picked it up and placed it on top of the chair, and climbed up again. Now, he was just tall enough.

Mrs Rabbit suddenly looked up and said sharply, "Tasseltip, what are you doing?"

"I'm just trying to reach this vase," said Tasseltip.

Then came a loud crash!

9

A very surprised Tasseltip sat on the floor surrounded by bits of broken vase.

Mrs Rabbit hurried to pick him up. "That was your own fault," she said. "I told you to wait and I would find you a vase. Now look at it."

Tasseltip rubbed his elbow which was a bit bruised. "I am very sorry," he said. "I didn't mean to be naughty."

"Well, it's a good thing that it's only the vase that is broken," said Mrs Rabbit. "Go and get a dustpan and brush and sweep up all these broken pieces. Next time don't be so silly. It's very dangerous to climb on top of furniture like that."

Tasseltip found the dustpan and brush and cleared up the broken pieces. When he had put them in the dustbin, he put the chair back in its place, and his stool back in its corner.

"That looks better," said Mrs Rabbit, and she gave him a large jam jar filled with water.

"Put your flowers in here, Tasseltip," she said, "then put them in a safe place until it's time to go to the Show."

So Tasseltip carefully arranged his flowers and put them on a table out of the way.

"Now, off you go outside," said Mrs Rabbit.
"I think your father could probably do with some
help getting things ready."

Mr Rabbit was very proud of his garden, and every year he took a large basket of vegetables to the Flower Show to exhibit. He quite often won a prize. Tasseltip found him busy digging up juicy, mouth-watering carrots.

"Hello," he said. "Can I help you?"

Mr Rabbit looked up. "Hello, Tasseltip. Of course you can. Look, there's a bucket over there." Mr Rabbit pointed to it. "Go and fill it up with water and then you can wash these carrots for me."

When Tasseltip had finished the carrots he had to wipe clean the longest runner beans he had ever seen. Then Mr Rabbit said, "I dug up the onions yesterday and left them on the table in the shed. Would you go and get six for me? Nice large ones."

Off went Tasseltip to the shed and found the onions. They were magnificent. He was very proud of his father for being such a clever gardener.

"That's splendid," said Mr Rabbit. "Thanks for your help, Tasseltip." He picked up the basket and went up the path to the house to show Mrs Rabbit. Tasseltip decided to go and find one of his friends to play with.

As he was going out to find his friends, Tasseltip suddenly remembered he had to put away the garden tools. He went back to do this, then set out again.

"I wonder where to look first?" thought Tasseltip. "If I go down to the river I might find Robert or Frankie, or if I go into the woods I might find one of the Squirrels."

Whistling cheerfully he decided to make up his mind when he got to the bottom of the garden. Instead of opening the gate, he took a few paces backwards and then ran forwards, taking a flying leap over the garden wall!

"Hey . . . Look out!" cried a voice. "You nearly squashed me!"

"What . . . Oh! Frankie, is that you?" said a thoroughly startled Tasseltip when he saw his friend. "What are you doing here? Are you hiding from someone?"

"Of course not, silly," said Frankie sitting up and yawning loudly. "I was just having a little snooze, that's all. I'm not hiding from anyone. What a way to be woken up – flying rabbits, whatever next?"

They looked at each other and started laughing.

When they had stopped laughing Frankie Frog said, "You nearly landed right on top of me when you jumped over the wall. Where were you going? Anywhere special?"

"Nowhere in particular. I was wondering where to find you or someone else to play with," said Tasseltip. "I was helping my father get his vegetables ready for the Show this afternoon, but we've finished now. What a funny place to choose to have a rest! We sometimes have a bonfire here to burn all the rubbish."

"I know it's not very nice, but I came to see what you were doing and I saw you were busy with your father, so I decided to wait. I sat down and I suppose I was a bit sleepy and just dozed off," said Frankie Frog, a bit sheepishly.

"Come on, up you get," said Tasseltip, pulling his friend to his feet. "Let's find something really exciting to do."

Off went the two friends up the path, skipping and jumping.

A little later on Tasseltip flung himself down on the grass. "Phew," he said, wiping his face. "The sun is hot."

"This is great fun," said Frankie. He had caught hold of a low branch of a tree which was hanging over the path, and was swinging backwards and forwards on it.

"Can I have a go?" cried Tasseltip, scrambling to his feet.

"Come and try, then," said Frankie, getting off.

"I say, Frankie, can you hear a strange noise?" said Tasseltip. "What can it be?"

"I don't know," replied Frankie, just as puzzled.

At that moment Mr Spiney Hedgehog came around the corner pushing an old green wooden wheelbarrow which was bursting at the seams. It was laden to the brim with flowers and vegetables.

"I expect old grumpy is on his way to the Show," whispered Frankie. "He usually wins a prize."

"Sssh, don't let him hear you," whispered back Tasseltip. "You know how cross he can get."

They watched Mr Hedgehog struggling with the wheelbarrow, and when he drew near to the two friends Tasseltip said, "Good morning, Mr Hedgehog. Isn't it a lovely day?"

But Mr Hedgehog was being grumpy. He was either pretending to be deaf or was in a very bad temper because he pushed his barrow past Tasseltip and Frankie without saying a word.

"Grumpy old thing!" said Frankie.

"I quite agree with you," said Tasseltip, and he was just about to turn his back when he said, "Look, Frankie, look what has happened!"

Frankie Frog turned around quickly and saw that the wheel of the barrow had suddenly broken off.

All the flowers and vegetables had tumbled out in every direction and Mr Spiney Hedgehog was sitting in the middle of them. He looked so funny the two friends had to make a big effort not to laugh out loud when they went to his rescue. Mr Hedgehog didn't like being laughed at.

Treading carefully so as not to squash any of the flowers, Tasseltip said, "Take my arm, Mr Hedgehog, and I will pull you up."

Soon Mr Hedgehog was standing on his feet looking about him in dismay.

"A fine to-do. Oh dear, oh dear," he mumbled to himself. "What a mess. Now how am I going to get this little lot to the Show? I can't possibly carry everything. There's far too much."

He looked rather pathetic and Tasseltip and Frankie felt very sorry for him. They had gathered together all the flowers and vegetables, but the barrow wheel was completely broken.

"I'll go and see my father," Frankie said. "It's not far from here and I'm sure he'll help. Wait here, Mr Hedgehog. I won't be long."

Off bounded Frankie with Tasseltip following closely behind, leaving a bewildered Mr Hedgehog.

Frankie soon found his father and explained what had happened. "Ho ho," laughed Mr Frog. "Of course you can help the old scoundrel. You will find my barrow in the tool shed."

Tasseltip and Frankie pushed the barrow back to where they had left Mr Hedgehog, and within minutes they had everything carefully loaded into it.

"Hmph," said Mr Hedgehog. "Er, that was very kind of you both to help me."

He fumbled about in the barrow and then said,

"This is for you, young Frankie, a nice tomato, and here's a carrot for you, Tasseltip."

"Thank you very much, Mr Hedgehog," said the two friends together. Mr Hedgehog took hold of the handles, lifted up the barrow and trudged off.

From the woods Frankie and Tasseltip could hear sounds of laughter.

"That's Susie!" said Tasseltip. "Come on."

He was quite right. They soon found Susie and her brother Friskie in a clearing in the wood. The Squirrels were busy jumping over a piece of rope.

"Hello, you two," shouted Friskie Squirrel jumping over the rope.

"Well done," said Tasseltip. "It really is high!"

"Well yes, it is quite high," agreed Friskie, who was terribly proud of his jumping ability.

"Rubbish, I could easily jump higher than that," said Frankie Frog rather boastfully.

The others looked at each other and Susie giggled. "Go on, let him jump if he wants to, Friskie. I bet he won't be able to do it," she said.

"Are you sure, Frankie?" said Friskie. When Frankie nodded he went over to raise the rope.

"Stand clear," called Frankie, and he went back up the path a little way. Turning around he ran as fast as he could and took a flying leap. Up, up into the air he sailed and just when everyone thought he was going to clear the rope, one of his feet brushed against it. He completely lost his balance, and down he tumbled, head over heels.

"You win, Friskie," said Frankie, getting to his feet. "You can jump much higher than I can."

Eventually they grew tired of jumping and skipping over the rope, and were lying down on the grass talking. Susie was making a daisy chain from a pile of daisies she had picked. "I wonder what time it is," she said. "I'm sure it must be getting late. Don't forget, everybody, we've got to take our flowers to the Show this afternoon."

No one knew what the time was, and Tasseltip said, "Susie is right, perhaps we ought to go home and get ready."

"Good idea," said Frankie.

"My father is taking my flowers for me. He is going a bit earlier so he can display all his vegetables properly. I've already put mine in water, so I hope they are still looking nice and fresh," said Tasseltip, scrambling to his feet. "I'd better make sure he doesn't forget them. I'll see you all later. Goodbye," and with a wave he went off.

When Tasseltip arrived home he heard his mother calling from upstairs.

"Is that you, Tasseltip? Hurry up or you will be late. I've nearly finished changing. Come along."

"Just coming," called Tasseltip as he rushed up the stairs two at a time.

"Go and wash your hands and face," said Mrs Rabbit, "and then change your trousers. Those are covered in mud. Your father and I have had an early lunch. He wanted to take his vegetables to the Show nice and early. I'll go and make you some sandwiches. Now don't be long," and off she bustled downstairs to the kitchen.

Tasseltip hurried about washing and combing his hair and whiskers. Then he changed into his new green trousers and tied a clean handkerchief around his neck.

As soon as he was ready he went downstairs. He was feeling rather hungry.

"Can I have my sandwiches now, please?" he asked his mother when he came into the kitchen.

"They are all ready for you on the table," said Mrs Rabbit. She was brushing her hair.

"You do look nice," said Tasseltip, with his mouth full. Mrs Rabbit was wearing her new dress of pale pink cotton.

"Don't talk with your mouth full, Tasseltip," she said, secretly delighted at the compliment. "Finish your sandwich and then we must go. I wonder whether I should take my umbrella just in case?"

"It's a beautiful day, I'm sure you won't need it,"
said Tasseltip with his mouth quite empty. "I've
finished now."

So they both set off for the Show, Tasseltip
skipping happily.

It was a glorious afternoon, the sun shone brightly overhead and they met lots of other people all making their way towards Deep Wood.

"I told you you wouldn't need your umbrella," said Tasseltip to his mother.

"You were quite right," said Mrs Rabbit with a smile on her face. "It is a lovely day."

"Oh, look! Isn't the tent lovely!" shouted Tasseltip in great excitement.

There, in front of them, was the biggest tent he had ever seen. It was bright green, and was covered in lilies of the valley, with variegated ivy trailing everywhere and pretty feather moss placed in clumps around the flowers.

Next to the main tent was a slightly smaller one with a notice outside which had the words TEAS AND REFRESHMENTS written on it.

"When we have looked at everything and the judging is finished I expect we will have some tea there," said Mrs Rabbit. "I am going to find your father now. Do you want to come with me?"

"Can I go and explore first?" said Tasseltip.

"Off you go then," said Mrs Rabbit. "You'll find us in the big tent when you're ready."

TEAS
AND
REFRESHMENTS

31

Tasseltip was thrilled. There was so much to see,
he couldn't make up his mind which way to go
first. All around the main tent there were little stalls.
A "coconut shy", "hula hoop" and his favourite,
"win a goldfish". Then he heard a band strike up,
and he rushed off in the direction of the music.

He found Tom Thrush's bandsmen in their
cheerful red coats playing the most wonderful
foot-tapping tunes. Tasseltip waited until the
music had ended and then decided to go straight
into the big tent to see what was happening there.

As he walked towards the entrance he saw that Mr Hedgehog was now sitting outside and taking the tickets.

"Ticket, please," said Mr Hedgehog, who was thoroughly enjoying himself being the doorman.

"Oh dear, I can't seem to find it," said Tasseltip, taking everything out of his pockets.

"Well, you can't stand here," said Mr Hedgehog. "You're blocking the way for other people. Go and find your ticket and then come back," and he waved Tasseltip away.

"I'm sure I *did* put it in my pocket," thought Tasseltip to himself. "I'll have one more look, then I'll have to go and find someone to help me get a ticket."

So he turned out his pockets again, but still he couldn't find it.

Tasseltip went back to Mr Hedgehog.

"Mr Hedgehog," asked Tasseltip politely, "do you happen to know if my mother is in there?" and he pointed to inside the tent.

"Now, look here, young Tasseltip," said Mr Hedgehog in a loud voice. He got to his feet and then said even louder, "The notice says quite clearly that you must have a ticket, so it's no good expecting me to let you in without one."

"Bother," said Tasseltip to himself. "Why is Mr Hedgehog always so grumpy? After all, I only asked him if he'd seen my mother."

He walked slowly away and then saw his friend Mr Mole coming towards him.

"Hello, Tasseltip. Isn't this splendid, and what do you think of the tent?" said Mr Mole.

"Mr Mole, have you seen my mother?" burst out Tasseltip. "You see, I can't find my ticket and Mr Hedgehog won't let me in."

"Mmmm. Let me see," said Mr Mole. "Perhaps you would find her in the refreshment tent. Yes, you go and look there."

"Thank you, Mr Mole," said Tasseltip.

Tasseltip walked up to the entrance of the tea tent and peeped in.

He saw Mrs Rat and she hurried towards him with a large tray of buns in her paws.

"Hello, Tasseltip. What's the matter? It's a little bit early for you to have your tea, isn't it?"

"No, thank you, I don't want tea just yet," said Tasseltip in surprise. "Actually I'm looking for my mother. Mr Mole thought he had seen her here. You see, I can't find my ticket and Mr Hedgehog is being horrid and won't let me in without it."

"Dear, oh dear," laughed Mrs Rat. "Never mind. Your mother was here helping me, but she went off to the big tent to be with your father."

"I'd better go and wait outside the tent then, maybe she will come out later," said Tasseltip, a little gloomily. "Thank you for trying to help, Mrs Rat. By the way, where is Robert?"

"Oh, he's in the big tent," called Mrs Rat as she hurried off carrying her tray.

Tasseltip was walking slowly back to the big tent when Mr Hedgehog caught sight of him.

"Come here, young Rabbit," he called to Tasseltip. "I've got something for you."

"Your mother and I have been having a little chat, young Tasseltip," said Mr Hedgehog. "It appears you never had a ticket in the first place. She thought you would lose it, so she waited until she saw me, and now I've got it," and he waved the ticket triumphantly in the air.

Tasseltip jumped up and down. "Oh! Does that mean I can go in now? Thanks, Mr Hedgehog."

"Of course you can," replied old Mr Hedgehog. "After all the notice says tickets must be shown and now you've got one."

But Mr Hedgehog was talking to himself because, with a sigh of relief, Tasseltip had already walked through the tent opening.

He thought that he would go to the vegetables section first, because he would be sure of finding his father there. He wasn't really looking where he was going and he suddenly collided with Susie Squirrel, who was coming the opposite way. They both sat down on the floor with a bump.

"Oooh, my head," said Susie rubbing it. "I was coming to look for you. Where have you been?"

Tasseltip picked himself up and helped Susie to her feet. He, too, rubbed his head. "I had a bit of trouble getting in. I'll explain later," he told Susie. "Are you all right now?"

"Yes," laughed Susie. "That's the second time we've had an accident today. I hope we have a bit more luck here."

"So do I," agreed Tasseltip. "Come on, I want to look at everything."

Susie led the way and they passed long tables covered in snowy white cloths and laden with the most delicious looking vegetables.

"Stop, Susie," called Tasseltip to his friend. "I can see my father over there. He looks very pleased with himself. I think he must have won a prize."

They both reached Mr Rabbit just in time to watch him shaking hands with Mr Hare, the Schoolmaster, who was one of the judges.

"Congratulations. Well done," said Mr Hare heartily, pumping Mr Rabbit's paw up and down. "Those are the best runner beans I have seen in many years."

"Well, thank you, Mr Hare," said Mr Rabbit, who was indeed looking very pleased with himself. "I have tried growing a new variety this year. I must admit they have turned out to be far better than I dared hope."

Whilst Mr Rabbit continued to talk to Mr Hare about his garden, Tasseltip and Susie went over to the table and saw a large card which said —

RUNNER BEANS   FIRST PRIZE
MR RABBIT

Tasseltip went over to his father and said, "I knew you'd win a prize. You must be terribly pleased."

"Well, I must admit, I am," said Mr Rabbit, in his slow voice. "Now, have you seen your mother?"

But there was no answer. Tasseltip had disappeared. Susie chased after him.

"Wait for me," she gasped. "What's wrong? Where are you going?"

"To look at the flowers in the Wild Flowers Competition," answered Tasseltip.

"Look – it must be over there, where that poster says Children's Section."

They stood in front of another long table with a white cloth. It was covered with bowls and vases of flowers of all shapes and sizes. Right in the middle was a very large bowl full of multi-coloured flowers, and a big card beside it.

"Oh, Tasseltip, look!" cried Susie, jumping for joy.

The card said –

CHILDREN'S FLOWERS   FIRST PRIZE
SUSIE SQUIRREL

CHILDREN'S

CHILDREN'S
FLOWERS
1st PRIZE
Susie
Squirrel

43

"Well done, it's a wonderful display of flowers, Susie," said Tasseltip to his friend. Susie looked radiant, her eyes were bright with excitement.

"Thank you, Tasseltip," she said, reading over and over again the card with her name on it.

SUSIE SQUIRREL   FIRST PRIZE

Tasseltip tried very hard not to look too disappointed. In as cheerful a voice as he could muster he said, "I wonder who got second and third prizes? I think I'll go and look."

He walked slowly along the table and looked at all the flowers. "Robert has won second prize," he called to Susie, reading the card, "and Friskie has won the third. Your parents will be terribly pleased."

Tasseltip was trying very hard not to show how despondent he felt. He leant against the table and in a quiet voice he said, "I wonder what has happened to my flowers? Perhaps Father forgot to bring them. No, I'm sure he didn't because I looked at the table when I got home and there was nothing on it. Oh well, never mind. I'll see you later, Susie."

He was just about to walk away when he heard her say, "Go and look at the bottom of the table, Tasseltip."

He was surprised, but did as he was told. He walked down to the bottom of the table and couldn't believe his eyes. There, on a pedestal, but still in the old jam jar his mother had given him, was his bunch of wild flowers. Next to them was a large card which said –

SPECIAL PRIZE
FOR VERY UNUSUAL FLOWERS
TASSELTIP RABBIT

Tasseltip pinched himself to see whether he was awake. "I don't think I'm dreaming," he said.

Mr Hare came over to him and solemnly shook his hand. "You've been very lucky, Tasseltip," said Mr Hare in his best schoolmaster's voice. "Some of the flowers you have succeeded in finding are quite uncommon. That is why I and my fellow judges decided to award you a separate prize." He went over to the table and examined one or two of the flowers. "It's not often you find sneezewort or lamb's tongue. Did you know what you were picking?"

"Er, not really, sir, er no," said Tasseltip, feeling very confused, but Susie came to his rescue.

"It was worth me bumping into you, Tasseltip," and she laughed as she told the story of how he fell backwards into the rose bush, and how he then had to go and pick some more flowers.

"It was well worth it, though!" said Tasseltip.

Then he heard Mr Rabbit say, "Let's go and have some tea. It's to be my treat. Now, Tasseltip, that's enough, stop showing off."

"Oh goody, tea," shouted Tasseltip, and he skipped towards the tea tent.

Mr Rabbit had invited so many friends to tea that they had to put two tables together. Altogether there were: Mr and Mrs Rabbit and Tasseltip, Mr Hare, Mr and Mrs Squirrel, Friskie and Susie, Frankie Frog and Robert Rat.

"You may all choose whatever you want to have," Mr Rabbit told his younger guests.

"Mmm, this is a welcome cup of tea," said Mr Hare to Mrs Rabbit. "I really am quite exhausted after all the judging I have had to do this afternoon. A flower show takes a great deal of organisation, you know. Thank you, I will have some more," and Mr Hare passed his cup to Mrs Rabbit who poured in some more nettle tea. Tasseltip and his friends were having a splendid time. They drank large quantities of blackberry and burdock cordial through long straws, and ate plateful after plateful of sandwiches.

"It's been a lovely day," Tasseltip told Robert. "I have been so lucky, have you enjoyed it too?"

"It's been a smashing day," agreed Robert.

"Ladies and Gentlemen," said Mr Hare, standing up. "Your attention, please. I have a surprise for you. Will you kindly follow me?"

"I wonder what on earth it is?" said Friskie Squirrel as they left the tent.

"I think it's jolly exciting, I love surprises," said Tasseltip.

"So do I," agreed Susie.

"Is everyone out of the tent now?" called Mr Hare. There was a loud chorus of "Yes".

"Very well, we can begin," and just as Mr Hare finished speaking the sky was suddenly ablaze with the most wonderful, colourful display of fireworks.

There were "catherine wheels" pinned to every tree whirring around and around with amazing colours, "rockets" that shot quickly into the sky with a whoosh. "Roman candles" blazed away, and "golden rain" sent little showers of golden stars falling to the ground.

Eventually they came to an end, the last firework had shown off its magnificent beauty and everyone yawned, said goodnight to each other and made their way happily towards their homes.

It was the end of the Flower Show for another year, and for everyone, especially Tasseltip, it had been a very lucky day.

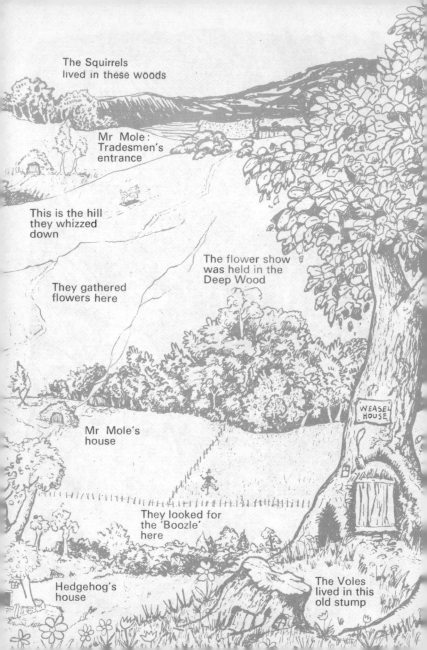

The Squirrels lived in these woods

Mr Mole: Tradesmen's entrance

This is the hill they whizzed down

The flower show was held in the Deep Wood

They gathered flowers here

WEASEL HOUSE

Mr Mole's house

They looked for the 'Boozle' here

Hedgehog's house

The Voles lived in this old stump